BULL

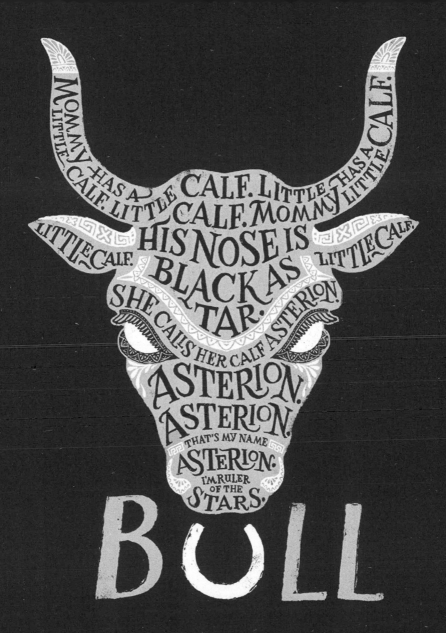

MOMMY HAS A LITTLE CALF. LITTLE CALF. LITTLE CALF. LITTLE CALF. MOMMY HAS A LITTLE CALF. MOMMY LITTLE CALF. HIS NOSE IS BLACK AS TAR. LITTLE CALF. LITTLE CALF. SHE CALLS HER CALF ASTERION. ASTERION. ASTERION. THAT'S MY NAME ASTERION. I'M RULER OF THE STARS.

BULL

A NOVEL BY
DAVID ELLIOTT

HOUGHTON MIFFLIN HARCOURT ◆ BOSTON NEW YORK

www.hmhco.com

The text was set in Fairfield LT Std.
Art and title lettering by Tegan White
Book design by Sharismar Rodriguez

Library of Congress Cataloging-in-Publication Data
Names: Elliott, David, 1947– author.
Title: Bull / by David Elliott.
Description: Boston : Houghton Mifflin Harcourt, [2017]
Summary: A modern twist on the Theseus and Minotaur myth, told in verse.
Identifiers: LCCN 2016014200 | ISBN 9780544610606 (hardcover)
Subjects: LCSH: Minotaur (Greek mythology)—
Juvenile fiction. | Theseus, King of Athens—Juvenile fiction.
CYAC: Novels in verse. | Minotaur (Greek mythology)—Fiction.
Theseus, King of Athens—Fiction. Mythology, Greek—Fiction.
Classification: LCC PZ7.5.E43 Bu 2017 | DDC [Fic]—dc23
LC record available at https://lccn.loc.gov/2016014200

Manufactured in the United States of America
DOC 10 9 8 7 6 5 4 3 2 1
4500642335

To Barbara,
my light in the darkness.

CAST OF CHARACTERS

POSEIDON, King of the Sea

*He may be a god but he's not
unreasonable, and when he is, so
what?*

MINOS, King of Crete

*All tender hearts despoiled, trampled, broken.
The king has spoken!*

DAEDALUS, The Royal Engineer

*Like a good dog, he is patient,
waiting for the day
when he and his son
will fly away.*

PASIPHAE, Minos's wife, Queen of Crete,
mother of Asterion

*. . . she named her boy
Asterion,
Ruler of the Stars.*

ASTERION, head of bull, body of a man,
a.k.a. Ruler of the Stars, a.k.a. the Minotaur

Fish? Fowl? Beast? Man?
Tell him, tell him if you can.

ARIADNE, daughter of Minos and Pasiphae,
half sister to Asterion

Minos calls himself a king
and her brother a monster.
She knows who the monsters are.

THESEUS, heir to the throne of Athens, future father of
democracy

In time, they all forgive him.

PROLOGUE

There beneath the palace walls
the monster rages, foams, bawls,
calling out again and again,
Mother!
Mother!

No other sound
but the scrape
of horn
on stone,
the grinding cranch of human bone
under callused human foot.

BOOK I

POSEIDON

Whaddup, bitches?

Am I right or am I right?
That bum Minos deserved what he got.
I mean, I may be a god, but I'm not
Unreasonable, and when I am, so
What?

Like I said,
I'm a god.
Reason's got nuthin'
To do with it.

But let's get back to where it all started:
Minos comes to me,
Mewling like a baby,
Frowny-faced, heavy-hearted.
He's got a hunger, he says,
A hankering, a jones, a thing.
But not for a woman!
This jerk wants to be king!
Of CRETE!
An island so dazzling
It could cure the friggin'
Blind. But it's not the friggin'
Scenery this friggin'
Minos has in mind.

Not the harbors or the shores,
The god-possessed waters.
Not the sheep, the trusty shepherds,
Their warlike sons, their lusty daughters.
Not the olives or the figs,
The sacred, long-lived trees.
Not the amber honey
Or the honey-making bees.
Not the thyme-drunk lovers
Who sigh among its flowers.

No,
All this clown wants
Is a little power.
He's got an appetite for obedience,
But no imagination.
And he doesn't ask for much —
Just his own private nation.

So he wonders
If I'd give the people
An omen,
A sign,
Something impressive,
He says, something divine.
Anything to prove
He's the man
For the royal job.

So what the fuck, I think.
I'm gonna help this slob.

Why not?
I got plenty o' nifty tricks
Up this metaphorical sleeve.
And you mortals?
You're ready to believe
Anything to prove
A god's on your side.
Besides, I got no dog in this fight.
No skin off my hide.
So, I wave my trusty trident;
Ain't nuthin' for me.
And abra-cadabra!

A milk-white bull
Comes walking
Out of the wine-dark sea.

The oldest trick in the book!
A piece o' cake.
But it doesn't take
Much to bring you
Mortals to your knees.

Yeah, you're hard to respect
But easy to please.

So Minos gets it all—
The palace, the power.
Big Man on Knossos.
Man of the Hour.

But all of a sudden,
He won't play nice.

Look,
He was supposed to sacrifice
That bull
To me!
Poseidon, baby!
King of the Sea!
Tamer of Horses!
Old Earth-Shaker!
And one helluva troublemaker
When some jerk shirks
His responsibility and
Won't keep his word.

So this Minos,
This "king,"
This two-faced
Turd,
Hid my bull and
Sacrificed another.

Like I'm some kind of mark!
A pigeon!
His younger brother!
A harebrain!
An idiot!
A jamook!
A snot-nosed kid!

The guy's all ego.

BUT I'M ALL ID.

I could have turned his eyes
Into a nest for seething wasps.
I could have turned his face
Into a snapping clam.
I could have given him hooves
Or studded the roof
Of his mouth with thorns.
Could have fitted him with horns.
Flippers.
Feathers.
Fits.
Made him smell like an outhouse.
Covered him with zits.
Turned his arms into eels.
His teeth into snails.
Bleat like a sea cow.
Blow like a whale.
Boils!
Scabs!
Gills!
A snout!
Turned his
Ding-dong
Inside
Out!
I could have.

But I didn't.

Parlor games.
A touch too mild.
Child's play.
And Poseidon's no child.

He needed something
He'd remember
His whole stinkin' life.
That's why I bypassed him . . .

And went after his wife.

When you play with the gods,
You're playing fast and loose.
Enough small talk—
I've got a sea nymph to seduce.

DAEDALUS

It was disgusting!
    The royal nerve of her!
I said, "Look, Your Highness,
    I'm an engineer. Not a pornographer."

And she said, "Look, Daedalus,
    I'm the queen, Minos's wife.
It all belongs to me,
    including your life,

which if you want to keep,
    you'll do what I ask.
It isn't much,
    this little task

I have in mind. Build me
    a cow of wood and hide.
Life-size but hollow.
    Then I'll crawl inside

and . . ." Her voice trailed away.
    No need to say more.
We all knew what she wanted.
    That unnatural whore

was the talk of the island!
    The way she raved
in the palace, begging . . .
    Desperate. Depraved.

She had no regard
    for reputation or rank.
But that's not the worst part.
    Let me be frank:

It wasn't her husband she wanted.
    No such luck.
It was Poseidon's Bull
    she was begging to— Look,

I'm *not* uptight.
    To each his own and all that.
But this was too much!
    I should have flat-

out said no.
    I won't do it.
But she was the queen.
    In the end, I said screw it

and I built the thing
       to her sordid specifications.
The rest I'll leave
       to your imaginations.

POSEIDON

I couldn't help but overhear
That pansy's harangue.
So, yeah—I gave the queen a thing
For the white bull's thang.
Be glad that I did!
If I hadn't? No story.
You know the drill:
No guts. No glory.

Now you're grossed out?

Well, life's not for wimps.
Sometimes gods are gods
And sometimes they're pimps.

PASIPHAE

You want me to feel
ashamed point
fingers blame
the god responsible
for that beastly
possession

but you'll get no
apology
from me no tears
no confession.

I know what I
know I know what
I see none of you
is that different

from me.

POSEIDON

No apology from the queen?
No shame? No regret?
Frankly, I'm a little hurt I didn't get
Credit for my work.
Oh well,
I won't complain.
I'm not yet done jerking
Her chain.
So let her get it off her chest.
A god who laughs
Last is a god
Who laughs best.

But let's keep the narrative going.
We'll skip the part when the queen starts showing,
And—
Oh, didn't I mention it?
That horny
Unnatural
Perverted
Coitus
Produced
An unnatural
Even hornier
Fetus.

Yes!
A calf in the oven!
Eating for two!
Let's shout,
"Congratulations!"
Let's holler, "Moo!"

Her labor, I hear, was excruciating.
With all the pushing, contracting, dilating,
They say the queen swore
Like a red-faced barbarian.
(If it were me, I'd have had a cesarian.)

But I won't be surprised,
Now the thing is born,
If Pasiphae hasn't
Completely foresworn
Her unqueenly defiance
And replaced it
With some wifely
Compliance.

Children change us; I ought to know,
Having somewhere, oh,
Over a hundred, more or less.
(Some are terrific; some are a mess.)

But let's see if Pasiphae's changed her tune.
Either way, I'm over the moon.

Oh, forgot to say,
For what it's worth,
I don't think
They announced
The birth.

PASIPHAE

They said it was all a dream I remember
murmured imprecations of the midwives afraid
to leave afraid to stay their
mournful ululations silenced
by the sudden bellow of his first
breath as if the birth were taking
place in a stable or a herdsman's
rough shack when I was back
to myself I held him
saw the blaze star-
shaped that marked his forehead points
separating his eyes terrified I named him
Asterion Ruler of the Stars I couldn't believe
he had come from me was mine carried
him nine long months my sacred
womb the secret room where he formed
ten little fingers ten little toes nails
soft and translucent his neck
already strong the heavy-horned head
shaggy the muzzle the long sensitive
ears the strong pull
when he nursed the o-purse
of his lips the lap
of his rough tongue the bold

nuzzle of his leather
nose against my shoulder throw

him from the angry cliffs they said feed
him to the hungry sea they said set
him down in the dung of the fields
alone better the gods have
him they said but

I wouldn't
couldn't
didn't
they understand he
was my first my bully
boy my beautiful beautiful

monster.

POSEIDON

Well, I gotta say it.
This is turning out
So much better
Than I ever expected!
She loves the thing!
Perfect!
Though I think I detected
A wee bit of instability there.
It doesn't take a shrink
To realize a link
Or two is missing
From that chain.

Of course, I can't blame her.
The labor, the pain,
Etc.
Still, all that overwrought
Human emotion?
It's embarrassing.
The motherly notion
That her baby is beautiful?
The leather nose and all that?
Well, I've got a little
Something planned
For her bully brat.

But I'm in no hurry.
It takes some time
To let the punishment
Fit the crime.
Speaking of which,
The actual criminal's
Say in all this has been
Rather minimal.
So far, not a peep.
What's that creep up to?
Diplomacy? Affairs of state?
Well, I hate to break it
To my smarmy friend
But those royal good times
Will come to an end.
It's sad when a father loses a son.
But wait!
I don't want to spoil the fun
By putting the cart before the horse.
Soon enough
I'll make it worse
By putting that horse
Before a hearse.

MINOS

It's not my fault Poseidon's such a child.
The queen defiled,
and all because I didn't keep my word?
It is absurd
to think that I got off scot-free.
She paid. Not me.
Still, I feel a secret thrill, a dirty joy
in the whipping boy
or in this case the loyal whipping wife.
She saved my life
from Poseidon's lunacy, his pucrile wrath.
(It makes me laugh.)
There *is* one minor complication:
the abomination.
I'll let her keep it — for a while.
It makes me smile
to think how I might use that horned thing.
My name is Minos.
And I am king!

POSEIDON

So Minos thinks he's dodged a bullet.
I should give him my finger
And tell him to pull it.

What?

You think a god should be more refined?
All touchy-feely?
No bump and grind?
Never uncouth?
Pure of mouth?
Pure of heart?
Never belch
Or swear
Or scratch himself
Or fart?
Never
Bawdy
Raunchy
Racy
Rude?
News Flash:
You don't want a god.
You want a prude.
But let's jump ahead a couple of years.

There's been a lot of blood,
Perspiration, and tears
Around the palace
Since the freak was born.
Minos wants to put him out to graze—
An idea, I think, that's not so bad.
A boy should spend time with his dad.
But Pasiphae, still half-crazed,
Won't hear of such a thing.

It's enough to make an old god sing.
Not to blow my own horn,
But gods I'm good!

Now I'm in the mood
To hear from the product
Of that infernal union.
You know who I mean:
The one whose paternal
Identity is, oh, how shall I put it?
Questionable?
Hey! Let's ask his father and
Question-a-bull!

And that, my friends, should squelch the rumor
That Poseidon has no sense of humor.

BOOK II

ASTERION

Mommy has a little calf.
    Little calf.
    Little calf.
Mommy has a little calf.
His nose is black as tar.

She calls her calf Asterion.
    Asterion.
    Asterion.
That's my name—Asterion.
I'm Ruler of the Stars.

POSEIDON

Awwww,
The little tyke
Has learned a rhyme.
I'm touched—
Almost.

What?
You think I should soften?
How often do I have to tell you?
I won't go back on the plan
I've set in motion.
I'm POSEIDON!
I'M THE OCEAN!

There's hell to pay
When you cross me.

So wise up, fool.
Get with it, dummy.

And now it's time to hear from Mummy.

PASIPHAE

In his eyes
I see the
sun I see
the moon I
see the stars
and all the
tilted
whirling
galaxies
I see the
undiscovered
constellations
I see the
Earth I see
nations I
see soil and
root and branch
and leaf I
see fruit I
see seeds of
all that's un
imagined
and new I
see light and
the wan white

future I
see the past
and sometimes
in the middle
of the night
I see dead
ends and dark
foul twisting
paths awash
with the fast
and bitter
flow of
innocent
blood.

POSEIDON

That woman is definitely
Off her nut.
It might be genetic, or
It might be that rut
That set her off.
You know what I'm talking 'bout.
Wink wink.
Cough cough.

But won't his brutish manners
Finally get to her?
His snorting at the table?
The stench of his . . . er . . . manure?
Oh, it's easy to love the darling diminutive,
But I've lived long enough
To know how wrong it can go
When the soft-tongued pup
Grows into the drooling hound.
Then he's locked up in a cage
Or dropped off at the pound.

The boy's had a few playmates,
Palace whelps
Forced to pretend.
But in the end

They turned on him
As children will do.
Savages, really,
Brutes through and through.

Well, time will tell.
We'll wait and see.
But sometimes you mortals
Disgust even me.

ASTERION

Age 9

These horns are heavy on my woolly head.
My tongue is thick and rough.
It's hard to speak.
I can't stop hearing all the things they said
when they called me
Horny Boy and Freak.
Sometimes it makes me wish
that I were dead.
My mom says it's because I am unique
that makes them laugh and say those awful things.
Instead of horns, I wish I'd sprouted wings.

I'd fly away. I'd leave them all behind.
Then they'd look up
instead of down on me.
They'd stare into the sun.
I'd feel the wind
rising up beneath me from the sea
and I'd be happy
and they'd be blind.
I'd shout and call them names
and then they'd see
what it feels like when a story ends
by hating those who said they were your friends.

POSEIDON

What can I say?
Life's no bed of roses
For a kid who's different,
A kid with horns.
A bed of roses?
LMAO!

It's a bed of thorns.

But let's move this thing along.
He's older now,
Healthy, strong.
Most days he spends inside,
Discovering that it's better to hide
From the light
Than face its bright humiliation.
But at night,
You can find him in the fields,
Or walking on the shore,
Lost in meditation.

ASTERION

What I hate:
- Mirrors
- Hats
- The looks
- The King
- Light

What I love:
- The sea
- The sky
- My books
- The Queen
- Night

POSEIDON

The good news?
He's finding comfort in solitude.
And I'm glad that he's reading,
Because, let's face it: breeding
Ain't on his dance card.

The bad news?
He's already making lists,
The gist of which is, well,
It's not a good sign.
I'd be worried
If he were mine.

Then again, it could be just a phase.
All kids that age are in some kind of haze.

ASTERION

AGE 14

I wonder if I'll ever understand
What I am or what one day I'll be.
A fish?
A fowl?
A bull?
A beast?
A man?
A superstar?
A gross monstrosity?
Minos says I'm nothing more than Nothing.
Can Nothing take a form and call it me?
But Nothing is ever what it seems.
Watch Nothing laugh.
See Nothing cry.

Hear Nothing scream.

POSEIDON

Okay. Okay. It's sad.
But let's not forget the
Way the river runs:
The sins of the father
Are inflicted on the sons.

By the way, by now
He's the oldest of eight.
That royal uterus is clearly first rate.
And so I'd like to extend my heartfelt congratulations,
Especially since the respective copulations
Were "normal"—some might say boring—
Meaning the queen wasn't whoring around
With four-legged beasts.
Or at least she used protection
Against guys who look like Holsteins,
Conceived in dung and mud,
Whose fathers go by "Toro,"
And whose mothers chew their cud.

The siblings have their brother's eyes, but not his horns.
The first was born not long after Asterion.
Minos dubbed his son Androgeos.
The boy's an athlete.
A stud.

The leader of the pack.
A hottie.
A hunk.
A quarterback.

Ariadne was next,
A member of the fairer sex
And the apple of her father's beady eye.
A lovely girl, comely, shy,
But more to the point, as soon we'll see,
Just ripe for plucking
From the family tree.

Phaedra is the baby and the last,
Her unhappy fate cast the minute
She left that fecund womb.
She fell in love with her husband's son.
It blew up in her face.
Ka-Boom!

We'll ignore the others
And quit with the family dirt.
It's time to get back to that taurine squirt,
If you'll pardon the pun:
Our two-pronged protagonist,
Asterion.

ASTERION

AGE 16

My mother calls me Ruler of the Stars.
I watch my subjects,
shining high above.
In the loneliness of space
they burn, like fire.
They cannot speak.
They cannot sing.
They cannot love.
They cannot grant their sovereign's one desire,
To lay down this "crown" and live as others live.
I watch Androgeos and try
to be like him.
But a rock can never fly.
A stone can't swim.

POSEIDON

Hmmm.
Intelligent,
Thoughtful,
Surprisingly gentle.
But when his hormones are raging?
Believe me . . .
He's mental!

ASTERION

AGE 17

Fish? Fowl? Beast? Man?
Tell me, tell me if you can.
Man. Beast. Fowl. Fish.
I want. I long. I cry. I wish.
Beast. Man. Fish. Fowl.
Watch me dance. Hear me howl.
Fish. Fowl. Man. Beast.
I need a fix. I need a priest.
ROTS? LOL!
They're in heaven.
I'm in hell.

POSEIDON

Well, I'm sure there's a cow
Somewhere
That finds him attractive.
Oh, stop being so reactive.
What were you thinking?
That some ingénue
Would come slinking
Into his room at night,
Compelled by the force
Of his animal magnetism?
It's just that kind of optimism
A god finds so boring.
That sound you hear?
It isn't the wind.
It's me—

Snoring.

MINOS

Of all my heirs the one I love the most?
Androgeos!
That olive didn't fall far from the tree.
He's tough. Like me.
Then there's Ariadne. What a beauty!
She'll do her duty
one day soon and marry a great prince.
And Phaedra? Since
she's just a child, it's still too soon to know.
My feeling, though,
is that everything with her will be just fine.
Why not? She's mine.
As for that deformed atrocity,
just wait and see.
Pasiphae can't coddle him forever.
I soon will sever
the cord that binds her to that horror show,
and she'll let go.
I know the queen. She'll forget about him
and return to life
and me without him.

PASIPHAE

Ig**no**rant self
a**no**inted fool
he thinks he k**no**ws
me but **no** one
k**no**ws the hard tight
k**no**t of my heart

POSEIDON

Oh, I guess I forgot to mention,
There's been a wee bit of marital tension
Between the king and his spouse.
Big surprise,
Since one of them's a lunatic and
The other is a louse.

Minos has banned
Asterion from the palace
And the table.
He lives in a shack now,
An old stable (HA!)
Overrun with vermin,
Mostly spiders,
Rats, and fleas.

Wait for it now.
Drum roll, please.

Let's hope he won't contract

Mad Cow Disease!

ASTERION

AGE 17

Minos sent me to this shepherd's hut.
I spend my time here
sleeping,
thinking,
reading.
The solitude is sometimes crushing,
But he will not break my spirit.
My heart is beating,
and for now that is enough.
No matter what
may come, I'll find a way.
I keep repeating
that wherever there is life,
there is hope.
One day my fate will change.
Till then, I'll cope
with whatever plans Minos has for me.
So bring it on, O king!
I'll play my part!
It's theater!
A work of genius!
Classic tragedy.
A masterpiece of Melpomene's art.
Or is it Thalia's play? A slapstick comedy.

Whichever, catastrophe or farce,
The script, I think, needs to be improved:
I wear a mask that cannot be removed.

POSEIDON

Now don't get all confused;
Thalia is a Muse, one of nine,
Each of whom has her specialty.
Mellie's is a real laugh riot—
She calls it Tragedy.

Meanwhile, Pasiphae has finally flipped her lid.
She's completely off-grid,
If you know what I mean.
Just barely holding on.
She rarely visits her son.
Says it's her delicate sensibilities.
Says she's allergic to the fleas.
Says she needs a buffer
Zone. Can't bear to see him suffer.
You'll excuse me if I groan and— Oh!
Did I forget to say I told you so?

ASTERION

AGE 17

I cannot understand
where she might be,
The Queen,
my mother,
she who gave me life.
Was Minos right?
Has she abandoned me?
She is my mother, yes,
but first she is a wife.
Does she now believe
I'm an anomaly?
Her absence,
sharper than a butcher's knife,
hacks away
at what I thought I knew.
Oh, Mother,
why won't you come to me?
Oh, Mother, Mother,
where are you?

POSEIDON

Not to worry, chickadees,
Our Hero's not totally alone.
Fortune—not me!—
Has thrown him a bone.
He has a daily visitor—
It's Ariadne, his half sister.
She's both compassionate
And tempestuous.
But that's not to say
These meet-ups
Are incestuous.
She's simply angry at the way
Her brother's been treated.
She comes to give him hope,
To prevent his feeling
So utterly defeated
And to commiserate
About their parents,
Who, she says, are ineffectual.
So pull in your tongues, children.
Not everything's sexual.

It's interesting:
As a god I almost always find,
The more repressed the mortal,
The dirtier the mind.

ARIADNE

Everything's a fucking mess.
My family is clueless.
Minos thinks because he's king
he can do anything
he wants to. And my mother
has lost it. There's no *there* there.
Phaedra? She's a complete whack
job. And a nymphomaniac.
Don't forget Androgeos:
Obnoxious. Conceited. Gross.
Thank god he's off to Athens
to compete in the games. Then
you have the middle child: me.
Daddy's girl, Ariadne.
Sadly—

POSEIDON

Excuse me—I don't mean to interrupt
But that girl has up and got me so excited!
Finally! Someone besides me
Who has her dots connected.
Too bad she's also disaffected.
Typical, I guess. But also dangerous.
And that part about Androgeos
Went by too fast.
The boy's an ass
Thanks to his doting father.
Pathetic!
But he's also a jock,
Super athletic, so
Minos packed him off to Athens
To bring some glory
To the family name.
It's the same old story:
The father living through his son.
When it's all said and done,
The boy is expected to win
It all, from the shot put to the javelin.
But, golly gee, javelins are sharp!
I shouldn't harp on such things,

But I hope there's not an accident!
You know, excrement *does* happen.

Even to the sons of kings.

ARIADNE

(CONT'D)

. . . Sadly, there is only one
I love. It's Asterion,
Body of a boy, part bull.
Strange, but also beautiful
in its way. And none of us —
Pasiphae, Phaedra, Minos,
Androgeos, even me —
could match the nobility
with which he bears his suff'ring.

Minos calls himself a king
and my brother a monster.
I know who the monsters are.
Minos has my life all planned
out. I'll become some dull man's
wife. Go crazy from boredom!
His queen! Under his thumb!
No! I have a plan of my
own. I'm not in a hurry
but soon I'm going to run.
And I'll take Asterion.

Until then, I'll be demure.
Charming! Sweeter than sugar!
The perfect little princess!
No more and no fucking less.

ASTERION

AGE 17

So when Androgeos returns to Crete
Ariadne says we're going to stow away
on the boat that brought him here.
How sweet it is to think
about that happy day
when I can leave
all this behind. I'll cheat
the Fates.
I'll have my way
and say a last goodbye to all my suffering.
A stone can never fly.
But it can sing.

POSEIDON

Well, well, well.
The plot sickens.
This little ol' god's heart quickens
At such an interesting development.
Hooray!
But what's that old cliché
About the best-laid plans
Of bulls and men?
Oh, wait.
That's too, too sad.
I won't mention it again.

But hey!
What's that?
Listen!
Hark!
The strains of the lyre?
The song of the lark?
If my old sea-god ears aren't failing,
It's coming from the palace.
Someone's wailing.

MINOS

Androgeos! Androgeos! Androgeos! Beloved son!
Gone! Gone! Gone! Gone!
The ferric word that claps inside my belfry head.
Dead! Dead! Dead! Dead!

Reports tell of a strange, ill-fated accident;
he pitched his tent,
they said, next to the athlete's training field.
A javelin reeled
off-course and hit my poor boy as he slept.
The heavens wept
on that hateful, inauspicious day;
the clouds gave way.

So Athens now will pay the heavy price.
Not once. But twice.
Not twice but all the circling years
their bitter tears
will fertilize the fields. My golden boy.
My heart. My joy.
Your bright blood spilled on thirsty mainland dust.
Your muscled chest
split open. Your beating heart exposed. Obscene
day. While that fiend

from hell, that freak, that horned and mewling devil
thrives. What evil
god allows such dreadful, dark perversity?
Hear now from me!
It's eye for eye! It's bone for broken bone.

With one horned stone
I'll be avenged and kill two birds.
Mark now my words!
Call Daedalus — that useless, sycophantic engineer —
and bring him here!

POSEIDON

Eyewitnesses report the spear
Was almost to ground
When a sudden wind found the weapon
And drove it on ahead,
As if a god's invisible hand, they said,
Was guiding it toward the sleeping boy's tent.
Can you imagine?
I'm hell-bent on finding out
Who that nasty god could be!
Oh, wait a minute!
It was *me*.

But what does Minos have in mind?
One horned stone?
Kill two birds?
Two-thirds of what he said seemed
The ravings of a man in grief.
Was he just spouting off?
Cathartic relief?
Or does he really have a plan?
Let's hear from Daedalus,
That clever, clever man.

DAEDALUS

I was sitting down to dinner
    when I got the call.
The king had summoned me
    to the royal hall,

so I put down my cup
    and pushed aside my food,
cursing both the king and queen
    and the entire royal brood.

Then I stood up from the table
    and without much fuss
hugged and said goodbye
    to my fledgling, Icarus.

He was quiet, the king;
    that's never a good sign.
His eyes were like a hawk's·
    when they looked into mine:

"You will build for me a labyrinth.
    A complex and riddled maze.
One entrance. No exits.
    You've got a hundred days

to construct it in the bedrock
    here, beneath the palace."
His voice so hard,
    his eyes so full of malice

that I stood there mute as dust,
    not uttering a word.
I simply shrugged and bowed my head.
    I didn't tell him how absurd,

how unfair, to bid me do
    this mad and senseless thing.
I am just an engineer.
    He's a mighty king.

Heavy rain began to fall.
    He handed me a drawing,
a blueprint of some kind.
    I heard ravens cawing

from their filthy rookeries
    and looked more carefully at what
the king had handed me:
    Circles within circles. My gut

began to heave. Circles.
    Hundreds. Maybe even more.

their diameters broken
    twice. Three times. Sometimes four.

I looked closer at the plan
    and felt my conscience pull.

At the center of the maze
was the image of a bull.

POSEIDON

Can you see where this is going?
You're probably upset again.
But you know me.
I'm crowing.

MINOS

The labyrinth will become the bull-boy's home.
There he will roam,
its paths designed to frustrate: twisting, turning,
his soul churning
in sorrow and despair. No books. No company. No light.
Eternal night
will be his faithful confidante, his only friend,
And in the end,
disappointment will ferment into a boiling rage.
Locked in that cage
the shadow latent in his nature will emerge;
then he'll be purged
of all his finer feelings, his delusive, higher aspirations.
Aberrations
in his character will take control,
and in his soul
he'll become the base, bloodthirsty brute he's always been!
And that is when
I will impose on the Athenians a heavy tax.
I'll break their backs
and I'll break their motherfucking hearts.
I'll tear apart
their loving families just as they did mine.

They'll pay a fine
each year—seven of their sons and seven daughters,
living fodder
for my masterpiece! The Monster of the Maze.
They'll end their days
in foul, unbridled violence and loathsome woe.
Let it be so.
All tender hearts despoiled, trampled, broken.

The king has spoken!

POSEIDON

Yikes!
Talk about your anger issues!
But if I were in his shoes
I might do the same thing.

Gods and kings:
It's best not to thwart us.
Humor our little whims.
Love us. Court us.
Light a candle.
Sing some hymns.
Shout, "Glory! Glory! Hallelujah!"
Then maybe we'll be better to ya
(If I can speak colloquially).
But let's drop this theology.

You'll excuse me if I gloat:
No Androgeos: No boat.
No boat, no flight.
Groovy, baby. Out of sight.

The would-be runaways
Are stuck,
Out of ideas and out of luck.

ASTERION

AGE 17

So once again I find myself defeated.
The Fates must laugh at my naiveté.
My dreams destroyed,
my foolish hope depleted.
Should I concede?
Should I go on this way?
Like Sisyphus,
abandoned, taunted, cheated,
a rolling boulder
crushing me each day?
They say that Minos has a twisting strategy,
a deadly scheme
whose centerpiece is me.

And now I've heard Androgeos has died
in Athens, where they say his funeral pyre
burned brighter than the sun.
May Charon guide
his soul across the Styx.
May he inspire
all those he left behind.
May pain subside.
May time console.

And may the searing fire
that scorched his muscled flesh and sun-warmed skin
cauterize this hopelessness within.

POSEIDON

Wah! Wah! Wah!

What a dunce!
He still doesn't get it.
If I've said it once
I've said it a thousand times.
When a god has been slighted,
Then the wrong must be righted,
And someone has to pay.
That's just how it is, darlin'.
Ain't no other way.

ARIADNE

Someone tell me what to do
about what *he* is up to.
I'm talking about Minos.
The labyrinth is now close
to completion. Daedalus
and his crew are working dusk
till dawn — dusk till bloody dawn!
And then poor Asterion
will be locked up inside it.
Minos is a complete shit,
but he is also the king.
What am I? A girl. Nothing.
Invisible. A ghost.
Still, I will do my utmost
to get us off this island.
Although everything I've planned
has failed so far, I won't stop
until we've left the hyssop,
thyme, the rank oregano,
all of Crete's stinking weeds. So
now I'll have to bide my time.
Life will be a pantomime.
Until I'm ready to act,
I will avoid all conflict
with the king, a counterfeit

performance, as would befit
a great and cunning actress.
Through deception, I'll suppress
my burning antipathy
for Minos. But one day he
will feel its fire. Until then
I'll play Princess Fraudulence.
Curtsey. Smile. Feign. Defer.

Look! The king's perfect daughter!

POSEIDON

That is one impressive adolescent,
But between us chickens
I'm not all that confident.
She is, after all, only fifteen.
Hey, here's an idea!
Let's hear from the queen.
Why don't we turn the page and see
If she's regained her sanity.

PASIPHAE

I

      know

   I

            know

I

    know

I

    see

        a

          dream

    remember

                        birth

            place

I

      held

          the

        star

                 terrified

    sacred

fingers

        soft

          translucent

                 lips

     the

lap

tongue

bold

angry

hungry

dung

monster

whirling

undiscovered

blighted

dead

bitter

self

no

no

no

no

no

no

no.

POSEIDON

Oops!

That ship has clearly sailed.

She's failed him, her firstborn son.

Speaking of that one . . .

ASTERION

It spreads like a disease,
like an infection
for which there is no cure,
no remedy,
no soothing balm,
no potions,
no protection
from its symptoms:
despair,
a bleak futility,
the loss of sleep,
the loss of all connection
to anything
that once was dear to me,
the loss of appetite,
the loss of all belief,
the loss of everything,
in fact,
but grief.

But my sister's optimism
is a wonder;
she believes
she'll get out us out of here.
She says she doesn't fear

the distant thunder;
a storm is coming.
The time is drawing near
when I'll wander in the labyrinth built under,
and where I'll start my new career.
No longer Ruler of the Stars,
but the Horrifying Hybrid:

Minotaur!

POSEIDON

Yes!
A storm approaches
So ferocious that even the cockroaches
Are hiding in their dark and secret spaces.
And with the tempest, all traces
Of hope seem to be gone
For our boy Asterion.
Lightning flashes!
Thunder rumbles!

That's

the

way

the

cookie

crumbles.

BOOK III

ASTERION

AGE 17

Mommy had a little calf.
Little calf.
What a laugh.
Mommy had a little calf.
His heart was black as tar.
She called her calf Asterion.
Carry on!
Carrion!
That's my name, Asterion,
Ruler of the

POSEIDON

Personally, there's nothing
I find less attractive
Than self-pity.
Yeah, it's shitty
What's occurred.
But why hasn't the boy learned
That life isn't fair?
Word!
It's true everywhere:
Fathers often destroy their sons.
Who do you think invented guns?
And if not their own boy,
Then any man's will do.
You don't want to hear it,
But you know it's true:
Genocide, massacres,
Killing your own?
That's bad mojo, girlfriend.
That's testosterone.

Even my own dad—
Now there's a story.
Is it fact
Or allegory?
You tell me.

It started with
A prophecy
He wanted to avoid
(Here's an interesting aside:
It had to do with patricide).
So he went on a diet
Straight out of Freud,
And gobbled up my siblings and me.
Except for one, the whole friggin' batch.
Opened his pie hole and down the hatch,
As if we were some kind of appetizer.

Turning your kids into fertilizer?
Talk about your child abuse!
My brother Zeus
Was the only one he didn't devour
And that's because at the last hour
Our mother hid him from our father's sight.
All day and all night I was trapped
In that foul digestive tract.
Until finally Zeus decided to act,
And in a move both filial and dietetic
Slipped the man a strong emetic
And out I flew like a freaky comet
In a spectacular stream of projectile vomit.
So you'll do your best to pardon me
If I come up short on sympathy.

Even gods don't get over that kind of trauma.

That time it was Papa.

Sometimes it's Mama.

DAEDALUS

First the queen, then the king,
    then the oldest princess.
To this crazy bunch
    I'm nothing more and nothing less

than a dog, something to pet
    and then command.
Roll over. Play dead.
    Eat from my hand.

But like a good dog, I'm patient,
    waiting for the day
when Icarus and I
    will fly away.

And that's not idle
    speculation.
Soon, we'll leave
    this stinking nation

on leather harnesses
    and wings that I designed
from whatever pilfered
    material I could find.

We'll take to the skies
    as free as hawks.
The king's loyal dog?
    He's actually a fox.

But for now our lives
    are not our own.
So I pant and run
    and fetch whatever bone

the royal family
    wants to toss.
Until we fly,
    they're the boss.

When Ariadne
    made her bold "request"
I had no choice.
    But now I'm stressed.

When Minos discovers
    his daughter's twist
to his own twisted plan,
    he'll be royally pissed!

And which of us
    will take the blame:

The princess or me?
    Oh, it's the same

in every corner of the earth:
    the powerful are
irreproachable;
    the rest of us are dirt.

POSEIDON

Now that's a man with an ax to grind.
He's got an okay mind
But his temperament's kind of sour.
I mean all that talk: power
And having to obey.
Then the bit where
He and his son will fly away.
You know, it just might not go
The way he's thinking.
In fact, I have
A sinking feeling
About that harebrained escape
From king and crown.
I'm talkin' 'bout physics.
If it goes up, baby,
It's comin' down.

But what of Ariadne's
Mysterious request?
We need to keep abreast of that girl
And what she's up to.
What has she asked the engineer to do?

ARIADNE

My brother's in the lab'rinth
wandering the obscene lengths
of its cruelly twisted
paths, his beautiful horned head
bruised on the unforgiving
stone. Nothing, no hope to cling
to. Only the darkness that
wraps him like a straitjacket
while Minos struts, a vulgar
puffed-up bird. Mother prefers
to take refuge in madness.
I don't blame her, I confess:
There's danger in sanity.

And so it was up to me.
I had to act. Do something
to thwart my father, the "king,"
and comfort Asterion,
give him a way to hold on.
And I was willing to bet
Daedalus had a secret.
Averting his eyes. Grinning
like a monkey at the king.
Always sure that his workshop
was tightly locked. So, I dropped

everything. I watched him day
and night. And very soon I
knew it all, his cunning plan
to escape on contraptions
built from feathers and beeswax,
wings that they'll strap to their backs,
lifting over the sea,
shouting "Ciao!" in the rosy
middle-fucking-fingered dawn.
All while poor Asterion
suffers in the contorted
maze. *Blackmail*'s a dirty word,
I know. But a girl has to
do what a girl has to do.
I threatened to tell the king
everything he was hiding.
The huge wings? The harnesses?
I'd expose it all unless
he gave me what I wanted—
his face went pale, then bright red—
a tiny hole in the wall
of the maze. "Impossible!"
he said. But in the end he
caved. Now, very discreetly,
my brother Asterion
and I meet each day at dawn.
We whisper through the tiny

opening Daedalus made, me
on one side of the lab'rinth,
him on the other. His strength
is overwhelming, humbling.
But what will the future bring?
How much more can he endure
when hope is an aperture
no bigger than the blossom
of the thyme? Won't the time come
when he will no longer be
my brother but the grisly
creature Minos has imagined?

That's why I whisper, "Depend
on me." I tell him I'll do
whatever thing I have to
to get us both out of here.
I murmur, "I'm your sister.
I'll save you. I have a plan."
He thanks me again, again.

ASTERION

My heavy step, my breath, my mournful wrawl
    echo in the maze. This, with the sound
        of horn excoriating cryptic wall,
            strikes terror in the rats that gather round
          me in the gloom, a winding sheet, a pall.
            Like a corpse, I travel underground,
          my sarcophagus a puzzle carved in stone.
          Like a corpse I live this death alone.
           I listen to my sister's tender words,
      as nourishing to me as milk or bread.
    They migrate through the void like fish or birds,
   blind envoys from the living to the dead,
to *me*, in this living rock interred.
   There is a plan. That's what my sister said.
    Asterion. She calls me by my name,
       and lights this sunless coffin like a flame.

ARIADNE

Ariadne means "holy
one." But how could that be me
unless prevarication
is sacred?

There

is

no

plan.

POSEIDON

So Ariadne's flying
By the seat of her thong.
Is it okay that she's lying?
I thought lying was wrong.
So far, it looks like her brother's survived.
But—poor little thing—
He feels deprived.
Still, I guess you've got to admire
The fact that he hasn't succumbed,
Gibbering like an ape
And sucking his thumb.
But you know what I'm thinking?
Deprived. Depraved.
Change one tiny vowel,
You slide from one to the other.
They're in a strange kind of consonance,
Like this sister and brother.

All I'm saying is Minos
Just might be right.
Deprive the boy of everything,
Food, companionship, conversation, light . . .
And all that deprivation could fester into wrath.
Then it's *Arrivederci,* Mr. Nice Guy,
Buongiorno, Psychopath!

MINOS

An emissary brought the news today.
They're on their way:
Seven boys and seven noble girls,
each raven curl
a-quiver on their fine Athenian heads.
Soon they'll be dead.
Just like my handsome son, Androgeos,
bemoaning ghosts
reeling through their parents' frightful dreams.
And when they scream
they'll know my anguish and my retribution.

This solution
increases both my status and my might:
All day, all night,
word spreads about the Monster in the Maze,
the dreadful gaze
that stops his victims' hearts, the blood turned cold.

If truth is told,
I started all the panic and the rumors.
They grow like tumors
and spread among the frightened population.
Thus, the temptation
to challenge me, to undermine my power,

is like a flower
plucked and left to wither on its stem.
And as for him,
the so-called Ruler of the Stars, the freak,
each passing week
wheels closer to the time his fate is sealed.
He'll be revealed
as the monstrous thing he's always been.
And that is when
the world will feel my potency and woe.

Let it be so.

POSEIDON

Man!
That guy's a dick!
But also so much fun
To hate.
Like all dicks, though,
He'll soon deflate,
And there's no little blue pill,
No herbal tea
That will restore his "potency."
Well, one man's dysfunction
Is a god's delight.

He *was* right about one thing:
The seven sons and seven daughters
Crossing my wine-dark waters
On the way to Crete.
Their parents think of them as martyrs.
Actually, they're meat.

Seven sons. Seven daughters.
Little lambs led to the slaughter.
They won the lottery.
Or lost.
The innards read.
The bones tossed.
And when worse
Finds its way to worse,
I'll repeat those lines
But in reverse —
The red innards.
The tossed bones.

The boys are barely old enough
To grow a beard.
But here's something interesting,
Maybe even a little weird.
One of those boys
Has volunteered!
You're familiar with the type.
Good shoulders.
Good teeth.
Believes his own hype.
And now, just to add a little fun,
Some folks say
That he's my son!
I guess it's possible, you know.
I've had so many one-night stands,
So many whams and bams and thank-me-ma'ams,
I can't keep track of every mademoiselle.
Plus, I'm not the type to kiss and tell.
Well, if I'm honest,
I'm not the type to kiss.

But truth is, his mother,
Aethra, was in a mess—
A sweet young thing, courted, prized.
Next thing you know she's spermatized
By Aegeus, who is King of Athens.
Of course. None other.

He'd been visiting her father—
And rather than be called a slut
She said *I* was father of her mutt.
(You humans tend to be less catty
When an immortal is the daddy.)
So in fact the boy's a prince.
And since he was born under a lucky star,
He says he'll slay the Minotaur.
Slay, says he, instead of *kill,*
But that's just some fancy diction
To disguise the bloodthirst in his will.

His name is Theseus.
Not yet twenty
But he's already thrust his trusty sword
Through dozens of your species,
Including fifty of his cousins,
A thug named Periphetes,
Cercyon, the wrestler,
And that sinner, Sinis.
Oh. We can't forget Procrustes.
You'll say those guys were villains
And you might be right.
But the thing nobody's willing
To say is how much
The boy enjoyed the fight.
How it buoyed his sense of self

To slice through neck or limb,
The spurting blood baptizing him
In the name of justice.
You'll argue he was just
Putting into practice
The philosophy of eye for eye.
Say what you will.
I don't mind:
But now we know
Why Justice is blind.

Still . . .
The prince is not without
Some redeeming qualities.
He's easy on the eyes
And eager to please.

Whatevs.

He will step soon onto Cretan sand
Unflinching, smiling, handsome, tanned.
Does the Ruler of the Stars
Stand a chance against such brutal confidence?
And what about his plucky sister?
Will Ariadne save the day?

Or might it go another way?
So shut your mouth and shut the door!
It's Theseus vs. Minotaur!
Who'll be stabbed?
Who'll be gored?
Virtue is its own reward.
A showdown's on its way.
No doubt.
And for someone, it will be
Lights Out.

Whatevs.

ARIADNE

It came to me suddenly:
That little man is the key,
the engineer, Daedalus.
He knows the maze, knows each truss,
each twist and turn, each channel
snaking its way through the hell
that my brother is trapped in.
It's his art, his construction.
He must know of a way through,
some clandestine avenue
or confidential thoroughfare
that will lead to light. And air.
He will tell me everything
or that sad escape he clings
to is dead in the water.
If I know him, he'll defer
to reason and tell me what
I think he knows: the exit
from that fetid, foul abyss.
He'll become my accomplice,
and in the yellow-robed dawn
I will save Asterion.

But I have to act quickly.
Each passing day it's clear he

is deteriorating.
And now the son of a king
is on his way to kill him,
kill my brother in the dim
halls of the labyrinth, where
his last thought will be *Sister,*
you failed me. How can I live
knowing that's true? Repulsive
pornographic visions fill
my dreams. Murderous, dreadful
scenes of violence and blood,
Asterion dead, slaughtered
by an Athenian prince.
The death of all innocence.
If those dreams are prophetic,
if their odious and sick
obscenities come to be,
what then for Ariadne?

POSEIDON

"What then for Ariadne?"
"How can I live
knowing that's true?"
I don't know about you,
But to me that don't sound good.
Maybe we should call a hotline.
But it's such a yummy plot line . . .
Let's wait.
We'll see what happens next.
As one dot connects to the other,
She will or will not save her brother.
Je m'en fous.
Still, you've got
To admit she's intrepid.
But what was that she said
About his "deteriorating"?
And why do I feel like singing?

ASTERION

I prowl
    the senseless alleys
       of the maze
           in darkness
               and asphyxiating
                    solitude.
                        Days are nights
                          and nights
                              and nights
                                  are days.
                         Where is the sun?
                            The moon?
                       The sky?
                    I am pursued
            by Furies.
        Their names
     are Mischief and Malaise
and into every
      memory and thought
          intrude.
              They whisper
                as I perseverate
                and roam
                     that in the
              labyrinth

I am

at last

at home.

POSEIDON

My, my!
That does sound serious.
He's almost delirious,
But let's not give up yet.
The sun still hasn't set
On this grim tale of grief.
Of course, as its chief
Architect, I know how it ends.
But this river has more bends
Before it flows into the sea.
So I'll forgo my omnipotence
And keep you in the dark.
Oooooo! What suspense!
I just love being me!

DAEDALUS

That girl's as dangerous
    as a viper in the garden.
How does someone so young
    come to be so hardened?

She showed up here again.
    Her insinuations, her threats
her degrading demeanor,
    her affectation, her epithets

even her sneering condescension
    meant nothing to me.
I'm a quick learner;
    I'm as hardened as she.

Of course I told her.
    What do I care?
Soon, Icarus and I
    will be in the air

like the gulls sailing over
    the loud-roaring sea.
Just father and son.
    Liberated. Free

from the demeaning demands
    of the royal family.
Minos, Pasiphae,
    their cruel daughter, Ariadne.

I said to her, "Seek out
    a length of woolen twine,
walk into the maze,
    let it unwind,

until finding your brother
    at the labyrinth's center.
Then follow it out
    the way you entered."

No secret passageways.
    No fiendish design.
No smoke or mirrors.
    Nothing but twine.

Nothing but twine!
    It's almost laughable.
Like a boy born with horns,
    half man and half bull.

POSEIDON

Nothing but twine?
Well, who'd a thunk it?
Gimme a doughnut
And tell me to dunk it!
Got to admit
That I'm impressed.
Sometimes the simplest way
Is best.

ARIADNE

Nothing but twine. What a fool
I've been. A trick so simple
a child could have figured it
out. I wanted to scream, spit
in that smug engineer's face.
If there were any justice,
any goodness, *he* would be
lost in the obscenity
he made, not Asterion.
He and that self-righteous con
man, my gentle, good father
the king, Minos, connoisseur
of hate, enemy of love.
But it's childish to think of
these things. There *is* no justice.
No goodness. No truth. This is
what they taught me, the awful
lesson that I've learned. This wool
will lead me to my brother.
Whatever else may occur,
he'll be freed from his ordeal
and the king's plan will crumble.

But this simple ball of twine
will never mend what's broken.
I've just told Asterion,
he'll be free tomorrow. Dawn.

POSEIDON

No ifs, ands, or buts!
That girl's got guts
For days!
But let's check in again
With our Man in the Maze.

ASTERION

Strange gardens prosper
    in this fertile
          tomb their blossoms
open wider every hour I breathe
           their rank perfume eat petals
      from each withered flower despair
             and rage unrelenting
doom
        bitter brackish spoiled
                sour man

   or beastie
        who
can tell

       Horns.

            Devil.

Fury.

       Hell.

POSEIDON

Horns?
Devil?
Fury?
Hell?
Uh . . . I'm no OB/GYN,
No kind of physician,
But something tells me
That boy's in transition.
Never mind.
I meant to tell you this:
Remember that prince? Theseus?
He's finally arrived,
Along with that sorry hive
Of thirteen sacrificial goats.
(Don't tell me.
I know: Since I said *hive*
I should call them *bees*.
But I'm Poseidon.
I do what I please:
Call heaven a hell,
A ceiling a floor.
So if I mix my metaphors,
Grin and swallow.
I'm Poseidon. Not Apollo.)

Back to the happenings on Crete.
Minos is parading his young, hobbled victims
Through the old, cobbled streets.
His family is there.
By force. On display.
Fair Ariadne — even Pasiphae
Has been brought out,
Though she doesn't know why.
From the look in her eye
I'd say she's been slipped a mickey.
Hey, I don't mean to be picky,
But is she looking a little worse for the wear?
A little paunch here.
A little sag there.
Apparently, bull-love takes its toll
On the body.
Not to mention the soul.

The young Athenians
Are frightened, cowed.
But the handsome prince
Stands out in the crowd.
His oh-so-proud bearing.
His abs, his pecs.
See the citizens staring,
Craning their necks

As the comely prince walks by.
Both the women and the men.
You can see it in their eyes.
They lick their lips. They fantasize.
But everyone is silent when
He stops in front of the royal dais,
Bows to the king,
And turns his gaze to . . .
Wait!
What?
Why, glory be!
It's our own little princess,
Ariadne!
And oh my goodness!
What a surprise!
She's returning the look
In the young man's eyes.

ARIADNE

Am I put under a spell?
Without reason, I tremble
and cannot look away from
him. Defenseless. Speechless. Dumb.
My heart beats so rapidly.
What is happening to me?

ASTERION

HORNS!

POSEIDON

What's going on?
Could it be
That some irresistible god
Asked Aphrodite's minion,
Eros (a.k.a. Cupid),
To descend from above
And let his love darts fly?
Maybe I'm stupid (NOT!),
But my opinion is yes!
Oh, all right, I confess—
It was me.
(For you grammarians, it was I.)
But let's not be too quick to scoff.
It often happens, the lightning bolt,
The jolt *d'amour*.
Poor Ariadne.
You know, it's always the one
Who is most defended
That's likely to be the one upended,
Undone by the power
of Love at First Sight.

I for one am delighted
That there's some chemistry
Between the two.

I don't know about you,
But I like a little complication.
Nothing's more boring
Than the shortest distance —
The straight line.
Now, would you look at that!
Ariadne's dropped the twine.

ASTERION

DEVIL!

ARIADNE

I did not save my brother
this morning. As if I were
bewitched, I put aside my good
intentions when an aged
servant brought me a message.
Theseus, saying he'd pledged
himself to me. His fervor,
his fire, his loving words were
powerful as sorcery,
a cure for a malady
that I did not know I had
but from which I agonized.
He begged me to come to him,
saying he was a victim
not of my father but of
the sudden and certain love
that struck him blind and senseless
when he saw me. His distress,
he said, was unbearable.
His poor heart, he said, was full.
I sent away the servant.
Then, donning her cloak, I went
to him.

ASTERION

FURY!

ARIADNE

Oh, do not blame me!
This strange infirmity
has rendered me powerless.
Feelings I cannot repress
recast me. I am no more
Ariadne, but am her
shadow, her puppet, her doll,
without will, vulnerable
to whatever love demands,
wandering the borderlands
of my own transformed psyche.
I am lost. Lost, and yet he,
Theseus, discovered me,
no more the disbodied ghost,
angry, and cold as hoarfrost,
but corporal and aflame,
on fire with yearning for him.

He will save Asterion.
This he has promised me, vowed
with words tender, pure, sacred,
that he will enter the maze
and guide my poor traumatized
brother to me and safety,
his voice so gentle when he

smiled and asked me for the twine.
And I gave it — secure in
the knowledge that his love for
me is real — with a sharp sword
to protect him from the fierce
rats that infest the perverse
gloom of the place. Soon, I will
embrace my brother. The chill
of these days forgotten, gone.
And then my Asterion,
Theseus, and I will flee.
Three of us in harmony.
We will escape to Athens,
joyful, until the time when
he will be anointed King.
Blessed day! And everything
will be the way it should be.
Asterion, happy, free.
Theseus and I as one
perfect and holy union.

THESEUS

Ariadne! What a rack!
I knew I'd get her in the sack.
As for her bro?
He won't outlive me.
No sweat.
In time they all forgive me.

POSEIDON

Oh dear!
I fear things have taken a very bad turn.
Someone lit a fire;
Someone else is getting burned.
But she's not the first girl taken in
By a silver-tongued prince
With golden skin.
So, let's not cast aspersions.
This is just another version
Of a familiar trope.
Anyone can hang herself
If given enough rope.
As for Asterion,
He's waiting in the maze
For Ariadne to arrive.
In the dark
In many ways.

THESEUS

FEE!
FI!
FO!
FUM!
LOOK OUT, HORNHEAD!
HERE I COME!

ASTERION

What is this new sound
waking me from sleep?
Footsteps!
Ariadne's come at last
to free me from this dark
and hellish keep.
I am delivered!
The footsteps coming fast!
O Sister!
What great happiness we'll reap
when these melancholy times
are gone and past.
Sister!
Ariadne!
Constant.
True.
Walk no farther.
Let me come to you.

I call her name again,
but in reply,
another's voice.
Mocking.
Sharp and cruel.
He tells me that

my time has come to die,
that he is fire;
I am but the fuel.
He laughs and jeers and boasts
and says that I
have been betrayed.
He calls me Ariadne's fool.

O Sister,
what's this unholy game you've undertaken?
I run to him.
A monster.
Lost.
Forsaken.

POSEIDON

No need to see the boy's blood shed,
The wounded chest, the severed head
Left for the vermin and the birds.

Here then are his final words.

ASTERION

HELL . . .

. . . is not
the pushing of a boulder
up a mountainside
to watch it roll
back with broken back
and broken shoulder.

HELL is the numbing of the soul.

HELL is not an unfulfilled desire.
It's colder.

Nor the thirst
that takes its victims whole.

—

HELL is the freezing
scorn for who you are
that transforms a faultless boy

to Minotaur.

EPILOGUE

POSEIDON

Well, my work here is done.
Minos not only lost his favorite son;
He also lost his favorite daughter.
Ariadne, after the slaughter,
Fled Crete with her Athenian brave,
Whom—big surprise!—she forgave
When he told her Asterion was too far gone.
She pretended to believe him.
You'll excuse me if I yawn?
But don't get your hopes up.
No happy ever after.
He soon abandoned her—cue the laughter!—
And with his sword and conscience clean
Took the fortunate thirteen
And returned to Athens
The conquering hero.
Theseus: two. Ariadne: zero.

I also thought you'd want to hear
About that whiny engineer.
Those wings he built?
Guess what! They worked.
But Icarus, that little jerk,
Flew too high
And took a header.

Now he's dead.
Could not be deader.

Surprise!
It's time for a wee confession.
I think I might have given you the false impression
That I was calling all the shots.
That . . . er . . . for example, I gave the princess the hots
For the prince. Or that I guided that spear
To Androgeos's tent. But let me be clear:
I *did* cause Pasiphae to love the bull;
After that I sat back and did nothing, knowing full
Well that all I had to do was let
Human frailty run its course. From the outset
I was confident it all would go amok.
Of course, along the way, I had a little luck,
But really it was just me counting on you
To do the things you mortals do:
Ridicule.
Follow orders.
Stay passive.
Betray.
What a pity!
It could have gone another way.

What the—? Was that me?
I'm getting soft! I need the sea!

I miss its greens and blues and grays.
Its singing whales.
Its silent rays.
Its shipwrecks resting on the sand,
Undiscovered and unmanned,
Removed now from all history.
I miss the sea!
Its mystery.
Its kelp.
Its creatures.
Crabs and corals
Devoid of complicating morals.
Its secrets.
All its saline riches.
I'm going home.

Ta-ta, bitches!

A Word About the Myth

When a story is still going strong after two thousand years, it must be telling us something important about ourselves, maybe even something we *need* to hear. Therefore, in retelling the myth of Theseus and the Minotaur my major responsibility, as I saw it, was to stick to the architecture of the tale. I wanted to approach the story with the humility and respect such great works deserve.

In other words, I didn't want to change it. But I did want to explore areas about which it remains silent. One minute we learn that Pasiphae has delivered an infant that is half man, half bull; the next, we hear the boy is fully grown and in the labyrinth. But what of his childhood? Could such a boy have friends? How did his mother feel about him? And what about his half sister, Ariadne? Was she sympathetic? Embarrassed? Or simply indifferent?

Naturally, a story as old as this one has many variations. Some writers tell us that Aegeus, the King of Athens, had Androgeos murdered out of jealousy over the boy's athletic prowess. Others say that his death was merely an accident. Likewise, some versions contend that the tribute of fourteen young Athenians was paid every seven years, some say every nine, and at least one reports it was every year (the version I chose).

But in spite of these minor differences, the basic elements of the myth remain constant. Minos doesn't follow through on his promise to sacrifice the magnificent white bull back to Poseidon, who, in revenge, causes the king's wife, Pasiphae, to lust after the bull. The result is the birth of Asterion, the Ruler of the Stars, but also the nascent Minotaur. Meanwhile, to avenge the death of his son, Androgeos, Minos demands that Athens pay a tribute of fourteen of its finest sons and daughters. These he places in the great labyrinth built by the architect Daedalus (who also helped the queen satisfy her longings for the bull), where the ravening Minotaur is waiting. Finally, with the help of Minos's lovesick daughter Ariadne, Theseus, who has arrived from Athens, slays the monster.

All of these events you will find in *Bull*. All else—the characterizations; the relationships between the characters; their attitudes about themselves, their world, and one another; Ariadne's blackmailing of Daedalus; the hole in the labyrinth wall—is, for better or worse, my invention.

Finally, I feel I must offer an apology to Theseus, who went on to become the King of Athens and is credited, among other great accomplishments, with being the father of democracy. No small feat. But it seems to me that this kind of hero—privileged, self-assured, the perpetual heir to the kingdom, and not averse to violence—has been and continues to be lauded throughout history. My sympathies have always aligned more strongly with Asterion, a boy, unlike most of us, whose deformities lay on the outside, visible for all to see.

A Word About Poetic Form

Okay. A lot of words about poetic form.

For at least five years, I carried the idea of *Bull* around in my head. Wherever I went, there it was, like a stray dog waiting for me to finally open up and let it in. And I tried. Many times. But the doors remained firmly locked. I had the Prologue, yes, but I could not proceed beyond those first eleven lines. Then one lucky day, I heard Poseidon speak. The doors slowly opened and that stray poked his nose through. Each of us, it seemed, had found what we were looking for.

Kind of.

It soon became clear that others—Daedalus, Pasiphae, Minos, Asterion, Ariadne—would have to do their part in telling the story. But how? They all couldn't speak like the free-wheeling and treacherous God of the Sea. The best way to do this, I thought, would be to employ particular poetic forms that would help readers differentiate and identify each character. I wish I could say that in selecting those individual forms I applied highfalutin criteria based on extensive knowledge of prosody. But the truth is, choosing the forms was as much impulse as anything else.

Like a prankster thumbing through the telephone book, looking for the name of his next victim, I thumbed through Miller Williams's excellent *Patterns of Poetry,* until I landed on a form that seemed, well, kind of fun. I'd never worked with any of these forms before—if I'm honest, I'd say I had never *heard* of any of these forms before—but as naive as it sounds in hindsight, I was surprised and delighted by the way the various forms shaped and guided each character. In a very real way, those forms wrote the book. Impulse, as is often the case, might have been a reliable guide.

Throughout, I tried as best I knew how to adhere to the forms' strict conventions. This proved to be as liberating as it was restrictive. However, since meaning must always come before form, there are occasions (not many, I hope) when I allowed myself a looser interpretation. When, for example, Minos is mourning the death of Androgeos, that second line of the couplet has four accented beats instead of the two the form dictates. In thinking about this now, it seems appropriate. Grief has upended propriety even in verse.

Androgeos! Androgeos! Androgeos! Beloved son!
Gone! Gone! Gone! Gone!
The ferric word that claps inside my belfry head.
Dead! Dead! Dead! Dead!

Here is a brief rundown of the forms as I understand them.

- **ASTERION.** At first, I tried the sonnet for Asterion. But he just didn't seem to like it. However, he did take to the *ottava rima*. This is an Italian form. Eight lines of iambic pentameter with a rhyme scheme of abababcc. Like a sonnet but six lines shorter. This seemed to infuse his character with the nobility I was hoping the sonnet would bring, but avoided, I hope, his appearing insufferable. On the page, though, the form looked too stilted and, to my eye, caused the poems to be read a little too strictly according to line. To solve this problem, I tried to contemporize the form by changing where the lines break. With two exceptions, the *ottava rima* is Asterion's go-to form.

- **ARIADNE.** The form is Welsh and is spelled *cywdd*. That should have tipped me off right there. Couplets of seven-syllable lines. But the trick is only one of the end rhymes can be stressed. For example, "Everything's a fucking **mess**./My family is clue*less*./" The lucky thing was that it gave Ariadne a young, contemporary feel. The unlucky thing was she was very chatty. By the way, *cywdd* is pronounced "cu'with." (Oh, those Welsh!)

- **DAEDALUS.** This form may have a name, but I don't know what it is. Four-line stanzas of two or three accented feet per line with a rhyme scheme of abcb. Kind of straightforward, as we might expect an engineer (as he is described in *Bull*) to be.

- **MINOS.** The king's form is English: the split couplet. One line of iambic pentameter followed by one line of two beats. As maddening as this sometimes was, those two beats were very helpful. I often was able to use them to allow Minos his kingly-sounding decrees.

- **PASIPHAE.** The queen speaks in roughly syllabic lines, which often imparted a kind of unhinged, stream-of-consciousness feel.

- **POSEIDON.** Because one of Poseidon's chief characteristics is that he's changeable (like the sea), I decided not to restrict him to a form. But as I looked more carefully at how he spoke, I realized it is often in a rough couplet of uneven (he's also unpredictable) lines. The line breaks of his (many) speeches sometimes demonstrate this, sometimes not.

About the Author

Trained in classical voice, DAVID ELLIOT has worked as a popsicle stick maker in Israel, a cucumber washer in Greece, a pop singer in Mexico, and an English teacher in Libya. He began writing when his son Eli, now an adult, was a child, and is the award-winning author of many books for young readers, including the *New York Times* best-selling picture book *And Here's To You!*, the This Orq series, and a series of critically acclaimed poetry picture books, as well as several middle grade novels. He currently lives in New Hampshire with his wife, Barbara, and Queequeg, a Dandie Dinmont terrier mix. You can learn more about David and his books at davidelliottbooks.com.